Copyright © 2003 by Colin McNaughton

The rights of Colin McNaughton to be identified as the author and illustrator of this

work have been asserted by him in accordance with the Copyright, Designs and Patents Act, 1988.

First published in Great Britain in 2003 by Andersen Press Ltd., 20 Vauxhall Bridge Road,

London SW1V 2SA. Published in Australia by Random House Australia Pty., 20 Alfred Street,

Milsons Point, Sydney, NSW 2061. All rights reserved.

Colour separated in Italy by Fotoriproduzioni Beverari, Verona.

Printed and bound in Italy by Grafiche AZ, Verona.

10   9   8   7   6   5   4   3   2   1

British Library Cataloguing in Publication Data available.

ISBN 1 84270 301 3

This book has been printed on acid-free paper

LEMMY
WAS A DIVER

Colin McNaughton

Andersen Press
LONDON

Lemmy was a diver,
A deep-sea diver.
Lemmy was a diver,
Six years old.

Lemmy found a treasure chest,
A chock-full treasure chest.
Lemmy found a treasure chest,
Stuffed with gold!

But Lemmy had a rival, oh,
A huge and scary rival, oh,

A bully of a rival, oh,
Named 'Bully-boy' McCoy.

It was a tug-of-war, they
Pulled and pushed and swore, they
Scratched and bit and tore, they
Wouldn't give an inch.

And how do you suppose, sir,
The fight came to a close, sir?
Well, Lemmy bopped the nose, sir,
Of 'Bully-boy' McCoy.

Now Lemmy is a rich boy,
A *fabulously* rich boy.
He's lost the diving itch, boy,
But now instead –

Lemmy is a pilot,
A top-notch pilot.
Lemmy is a pilot,
Six years old.

Lemmy flew around the world,
All the way around the world,
Single-handed 'round the world,
Go, Lemmy, go!

Though many tried to race him,
And did their best to chase him,
No one could outpace him –
The leader of the pack.

The only person who got near,
You may not be surprised to hear,
Was 'Bully-boy' McCoy - oh, dear,
It seems his wings fell off.

"Hip, hip, hurrah, the prize is mine,"
Said Lemmy, as he crossed the line

In new world-record-breaking time.
But what will he do next?

Lemmy is an astronaut,
An outer-space-type astronaut,
The fly-across-the-cosmos sort –
Reaching for the stars!